Twice Blessed
The Special Life of Twins

by Patrice Cheviot

illustrated by Ann Rothan

WELCOME TO THE WORLD OF TWINS...

Life with a twin is so wonderful! Meet Christopher and Lisa, twins growing up together sharing a double portion of delightful adventures.

Share the carefree play times of two special children born within minutes of each other in this simple story of childhood innocence, friendship, love and fun!

Printed in the U.S.A. by American workers.
This publication is printed on recycled paper and with soy-based inks.
Through www.coolingtheplanet.org, Waterside Productions, Inc. replenishes more than the number of trees required to print this publication.

Dedication

This book is dedicated to my twin brother Cliff.
No words, actions, feelings or emotions could ever
express the immense gratitude and love I have
for him and for his being such a very special and
treasured part of my life.

I would also like to express my love and appreciation
to my wonderful husband and best friend Robert for
his confidence in me to write this book, for all his
encouragement, support and love, and for continuing
to be that special and precious part of my life.

WHAT MAKES A TWIN?

This story is about twin children, named Christopher and Lisa. Twins share many special experiences as they grow up.

Do you know what makes a twin?

Twins happen when two babies are born at the same time one right after the other. Twins are either two boys or two girls – or even a boy and a girl, and have so much fun because they are always the same age growing up!

Christopher and Lisa know how special this bond is...

Christopher and Lisa have their own language. They learned it before they ever knew "grown-up language."

To their mother and father and anyone else, it sounds like "jibber-jabber."
But these two understand each other perfectly.

One reason it is such fun being a twin is that you are never alone.

You always have someone to play with — there is twice the fun
and twice as much love!

FRIENDS

The neighborhood where Christopher and Lisa live is full of nice kids they call "their" friends. Before each school day, their friends come to pick them up and off they run!

Silly Willy giggles a lot and makes jokes – has freckles all over his face! Ken is very serious and has a stern look. Michelle is always cheerful and fun-loving - never minds when Christopher and Lisa come late to play.

Ellie is good-natured and goes happily along with everyone else's plans. Susie is a gymnast - always skipping and turning cartwheels on the street! Then there is Bobby - such a nice, positive fellow. Christopher and Lisa love them all and feel twice blessed to have so many friends.

"It's so much fun to be around our friends," they tell each other.

MOMMY

Their friends love to visit the twins' home. As they slip through the back door of the kitchen, the smell of delicious Swedish pancakes drifts up through the air...

Mommy is Christopher and Lisa's Swedish-born mother — always loving, smiling, and cheerful — with a twinkle in her eyes, ready to greet them with a big hug and hot bites of buttery pancakes smothered in syrup.

She loves making tasty treats of every kind and feels twice blessed to share them with all of us. They always taste so good!

"We love you, Mommy," the twins cry out with glee.

ON THE WAY TO SCHOOL

The children walk to school, and sometimes run. Their old-fashioned street is beautiful! Magical! Huge maple trees line each side in front of gingerbread-like houses. The early morning sun shines through the leaves making many colors — ruby red, golden yellow, apple green — as fairy dust speckles of gold fall from white clouds above. Brilliant orange and rust-colored leaves cover the ground. The children just feel like dancing!

Whenever Lisa runs too fast, Christopher warns her to slow down so she won't fall on the hard, uneven sidewalk.

"Watch out, Lisa!" calls Christopher. As she runs and giggles without a care, she sometimes takes a tumble. It's a comfort to know she has twice the protection that other girls have because her twin brother, Christopher, always watches out for her.

The children race to school, pushing each other into the crunchy, dried leaves to get a leg ahead. They get to their grammar school just in time, sit down at their desks, breathless with happy memories of their playful walk together.

BIRTHDAY PARTIES

Children's birthday parties are lots of fun — full of good times for all. As twins they'll celebrate their birthday together forever. That's something to think about!

Christopher and Lisa's birthday parties have twice of everything! Twice as many kids coming to the party, twice as many presents to unwrap, and twice as much fun! Two large birthday cakes sit on the table - one for each twin. There are two sets of candles to blow out — one blue and one pink. Birthdays with twins are doubly delicious because everyone gets to taste two cakes instead of one...and with lots of ice cream on top!

And the games! There is twice the laughter when they are playing.

"I'm better at hopscotch than you are," Lisa tells Ellie, but Ellie takes first prize at the party today and wins a bag of jacks.

Christopher's favorite sport is running relay races. Once he fell down and almost got trampled by Willie who ended up winning the race! His prize is a box of pick-up sticks.

The children also play "Pin the Tail on the Donkey" and "Musical Chairs," so everyone has a chance to win something. All the girls and boys at the birthday party get "goody bags" filled with candy, nickels, and crayons. It doesn't get any better than that!

PLAYING TOGETHER

On the third floor of the large house where Christopher and Lisa live is their playroom where they play for endless hours with all their friends.

Christopher's friends like different games than Lisa's friends, so they have twice as many games to play.

"Come on, let's go guys. You're so slow! I can run faster than all of you," yells Christopher, as the boys tear up the stairs. Lisa's friends follow them, but are not as rowdy as the boys.

No one ever wants to leave. It is always a great day to play together with the boys and girls in the neighborhood!

CHRISTOPHER'S TRAINS

What fun we have with Christopher's Lionel® train set, which is very special to him. We can hear the whistling sound of the train as we play.

Daddy built a **train table** for the set, with different levels for the cars and engines. There are loading stations for working cars, a train stop for people commuting to work, and even a train station for people going on a pleasure ride.

SUCH FUN! The train's whistle blows smoke from the engine and sometimes the smoke looks like a sailboat...or a dragon...or even a roaring lion.

STOP

LISA'S DOLLHOUSE

Lisa's dollhouse, which stands two stories high, is very special because it was made just for her by Daddy. Christopher and Lisa's Daddy feels twice blessed to build toys for both boys and girls.

Lisa likes how elegant the inside is – with mahogany and cherry furniture and pretty wallpaper and silk drapes made by her talented and creative Mommy.

"Let's pretend we're a big family living in this great house," Lisa calls to Michelle, Susie, and Ellie. We'll be a mommy and a daddy with two children. We can have breakfast together at the kitchen table, dinner in the pretty dining room, and then sit on the sofa in the family room, watching television.

They take turns being different family members. It is such fun!

RAINY DAYS

"Oh, no," says Lisa to her twin brother, Christopher. "It's raining outside! What are we going to do? We can't go out and play with our friends. And nobody will come over to play with us in this weather."

"Well," says Christopher, "how about doing fun things here? Just the two of us. We can go into the attic and play ghosts."

That sounds like it could be fun, though Lisa is a tiny bit scared, not knowing just what Christopher means...

When they get upstairs to the attic there
are many closets. Lisa decides to hide in
a really tiny place. Christopher starts
looking for her, but she's nowhere to
be found. BOO! She suddenly jumps out
and frightens him, laughing hard at how
scared his face looks. Christopher doesn't
think it is funny at all.

"We're supposed to be having fun, and
that wasn't funny," he cries.

"Oh, Christopher, I'm sorry I scared you, but don't be that way. You would have done the same thing if you had thought of it. I just wanted to be a silly ghost."

Christopher grumbles and admits that it's true and suggests they play Dominos instead.

So, even rainy days are never lonely for twins because they always have each other to play with – right in the same house.

It's like having a built-in friend!

SUMMERS AT THE SEASHORE

Christopher and Lisa's parents buy a little house at the seashore for the family to spend summers. Can you imagine spending a whole summer...from the last day of the school year to the day before school starts in the fall...at the beach and in the water? For Christopher and Lisa this is "Heaven on Earth."

They both love sailing on the bay. Christopher is a natural sailor. He always knows what to do. Lisa isn't nearly as courageous as her twin brother. She pretends to be and puts on a brave face, but inside she's truly frightened and nervous. The strong wind creates many challenges for them, but twice as many hands on deck make for an easier trip.

Then they go home for lunch. Mommy has a cold glass of milk and peanut butter and jelly sandwiches for them. They clean up, change into dry bathing suits and hurry back to the sandy beach, where they play and swim with their friends for hours.

Their special friend and pal is the lifeguard. He remembers each of their names, and every year remarks how much they have grown!

END OF THE DAY

With the setting of the sun casting long, purple shadows, Christopher and Lisa know it is time to head home.

Many times after dinner a whole gang of children go to the movies. Christopher loves going barefoot. When he has to, he carries his sneakers and puts them on at the last minute.

Lisa's favorite movie theater is at the end of a pier out on the lake. Since there is no air conditioning, she likes hearing the water lapping against the pilings as she watches the movie. Though it is quite warm and humid, nobody cares. Christopher and Lisa are with their friends, and that's what matters most.

Oh, what special summers the twins experience!

No matter the time of year, the end of every
day is special with a twin because they are
twice blessed to have each other!

Epilogue

Patrice Cheviot

I realized after writing this story about Christopher and Lisa that there was one major theme playing through it all — the fun and love that can be experienced intensely in the relationship of twins. In this case, the twins are a brother and sister born at the same time, then growing up into adulthood.

Their story can be enjoyed by people of all ages, by families, and among friends. Everyone should have fun in childhood, whether they are born as twins, as siblings of different ages, or as an only child. Remember, if you don't have a brother or sister close in age, you can always have a best friend to feel twice blessed!

Thank you so much, dear reader, for taking time to read this story. I hope you feel the same love that I felt in writing it, wherever you are and whoever you are with today. May you feel the Love that is the Greatest Power in the Universe. We are all brothers and sisters, after all!

From a twin's heart, I wish you double blessings as you close this little book and continue on your path through life.

Love – Light – Prayers

Patrice Cheviot ♡

About the Author

Patrice Cheviot lives in Jupiter, Florida with her husband Robert. She is a certified holistic healing practitioner, artist, sculptor, musician, pastoral care and bereavement counselor and is currently writing books on spirituality. As a twin, Patrice knows the excitement and joy that sharing life with a twin can bring.

Artist/Illustrator

Ann Rothan is a renowned artist living in Fort Myers, Florida. She illustrates for children's books, magazines, publishers, and recording artists. Specializing in sacred art, she is a coveted nationwide speaker on spirituality.